The Three Tales of Kings

Robert Cristante

Published by Robert Cristante, 2022.

THE THREE TALES OF KINGS

First edition. August 1, 2022.

Copyright © 2022 Robert Cristante.

ISBN: 979-8201696474

Written by Robert Cristante.

Table of Contents

Lazuli and Kabuli
By
Robert Cristante

"Tell us a story grandpa." A brother and sister said.

Their grandfather said, "Which one do you want to hear?"

"The Magic Paper, please Grandpa." They said.

Their grandfather smiles, "How about a true story of Lazuli and Kabuli."

They replied, "Yes, please!"

"Well Lazuli and Kabuli were once two nations or more, so kingdoms do not like it is today where we live in peace. Kabuli was a bigger nation than Lazuli and war broke out; where Lazuli triumphed over Kabuli to brooch and reclaim their land. When the time for peace came between the two, I brought them together."

They listen on with excitement.

***

The head mistress of court etiquette was teaching the rules of being in the High King's presence, the three princesses had enough of the boring lesson of how they should be presented to their uncle. Princess Anna, the eldest of the three princesses at eleven spoke in a mocking tone, "Oh Mistress, why must we always listen to the etiquette as our own court is the same as our Uncle's."

Their mother, whom is sister to the High King, knew her place on the throne was not a woman's choice and should not hold reign over the whole Lazuli Kingdom. Her father wanted her to marry for power of land to the west of Lazuli. Of course, he did not expect his only daughter to fall head over heels with the King of the Waterfront of Lazuli.

As the Mistress keep going on about how to address the High King, she started to fume when she saw the three princesses had left.

Anna is the ringleader of the three, and when the middle child Leah, decides something she follows her own thoughts. The smallest of the three whom just followed Leah, Abigail adores her little Stinky – a small piece of cloth which she does not relent for the washing maids to clean it.

***

The High King stayed in his study for most of the morning, signing decrees and such for the kingdom of Lazuli. He was reading the sworn statement of a prisoner which he could not deal with. The prisoner was his lost twin brother and today was his final judgment. Even though Otto knew the moment he saw his brother ten weeks ago, the decision to end his brother's life is one he hated. The statement stated he was innocent, but all the evidence pointed to his brother. He thought, *if I put to death my own brother for a crime, he did not commit then I must find a way to prevent his death... a duel with the accuser... by God Jorge of Lazuli, I pray for your guidance in this duel.*

The Magistrate had knocked on the study's door and he waited for the High King to say enter.

As he heard the words, the Magistrate said, "Ye highest majesty, I come to see if the decree for the death of Prisoner X is signed."

"I have some more questions for Prisoner X, and therefore I will not be signing any decree of death." the High King spoke.

"The evidence is all in plain fact and witnesses have sworn to see the prisoner to be at the scene." The Magistrate said.

"Exactly my point, to be at the scene is no cause for suspicion of any guilt. And his statement does not convey with the other statements." the High King pointed out and then asks, again "Also you do not answer my question of the accuser. Who is the accuser?"

Just then the three nieces barged in, as the Magistrate said, "I cannot tell for he will make my life unbearable."

"You do not know how unbearable I can make you. Tell me the name of the accuser before I bring my judgment of Prisoner X."

The Magistrate bowed and left with no words, as the three nieces heard their uncle getting angry.

"Anna, Leah and Abigail why are you not with Mistress Rose?" the High King still angry from his last appointment, seeing his nieces quiet as mouse's, "Well!!!"

Abigail squeak, "Stinky wanted to see Uncle Otto."

This statement had made their uncle laugh, as he said, "I smell Stinky from here. If stinky is not clean by dinner tonight, I'll..."

Anna said, "Mistress Rose hammer us with the same etiquette as we learn from mother."

"Okay I see," the High King said, "that will not do. Has she taught you your letters, numbers and all those lady's things?"

Anna said, "Yes but I get bored quickly with it."

"Of course, you Leah decide that staying is no fun as well and follow Anna." Otto said, "and you my little one just follows your sisters."

Abigail had walk up to her Uncle and sat on his lap and she said, "Uncle Otto, please tell us of the three princesses."

The nieces have always liked their uncles stories, "No I will not until you finish your lessons and when you finish then I might decide."

Mistress Rose was furious to see her pupils were with the High King, she bowed and said, "I beg for forgiveness for interrupting you, Your Majestic Majesty..."

"Mistress Rose, it is not you who should ask for forgiveness..." The High King said, "It seems my nieces should be taught a lesson of obedience. I have the best course for they will do so. You Mistress will have to overlook that they do a good job. They will go to the kitchens and wash every bowl, plate and cup; and then polish all the silver."

The three girls looked shock at the punishment and the two youngers started to weep.

"You three should have stayed in your lessons with Mistress Rose. It is a just punishment and if you disturb me again, think of this punishment and remember the next will be harder than this. Off you go and finish of the lessons and lunch soon will be here."

The three girls said in unison, "Sorry Mistress Rose."

The girls bowed to their uncle, and Mistress Rose said, "Good and depart." As the girls left, Mistress Rose said, "Your Majesty, thank you."

The girls were filed in a straight line awaiting their teacher whom bowed and said, "Quick march."

***

Once the lessons were over the three girls went to lunch which their Uncle Otto had a five course lunch ready for twenty five Kings and families. Mistress Rose follows the girls to the dining hall where the lunch party had started. While the princesses ate and knew their punishment would start soon, the eldest ask; "Your magnificent majesty, could you tell the tale of your ascension to the throne?"

The twenty five Kings were aghast to hear such a young girl to speak, King Leon was ashen by his daughters' outspoken question; the High Kings' sister stood up with such a fury, the High King spoke, "Sister dear, it is okay. Princess Anna you'll have to work very hard this afternoon for the outburst. The Magistrate will need you to clean a cell in the dungeons. Well for that story of my day that I became High King. Princess Anna you see these men before you – even your father – became Kings that day, twenty years ago."

Otto started the story with the moment he remembered; the words he said as a young Chief-Lord, "Oh father you must fight the Kabuli. They are vermin on the field of battle."

"Son, yes they are but we are lions. We will fight but we do so as Lazuli's. This day I am to become the High King of Lazuli and free my people from the tyranny of Kabuli." Pauses as the different tribes looked on, "Lyon is my name and pronounce here to all my people of Lazuli, as High King of this land, I will fight to bring this land as ours. My young Chief-Lord as my son will be my heir to the Lion Throne. Thad, be the King of South of Lazuli; Manchor, King of East of Lazuli..."

Hail and to battle... someone scream as the pride of Lazuli and the vermin of Kabuli clashed in battle. The swords, shields, axes and spears were used to battle each other. The Kings of Lazuli were beside their High King, protecting each his flanks and if one was loss their sons took their place. I was behind my father protecting him, the circle of metal and steel, like a wheel the pride of Lazuli fought the Kabuli. Driving the vermin horde out of the lands and on the third day of fighting did the Lazuli's reclaimed their land. On that triumphant day their High King also died, I became the High King, the last words my father said, "Otto you must marry and must make sure your sister marry. Here take this sword from my chest... free me from this vessel to Jorge's Hall of the Lions. I can rest at the feet of the God Jorge."

I took hold of the gold hilt of the Kabuli sword, and pulled. With ease I freed my father from an unfinished death. The people of Lazuli spoke in volumes, like thunder clapping the sky, "Hail to Otto, the High King of Lions."

The same words escaped the lips of all the twenty five noble kings and family as the servants served the fourth meal – salad and fruit platters. High King Otto now held the hilt's pommel of the sword, as Princess Anna stood and said, "Well Uncle Otto is that the sword you hold now."

Ignoring the slight personal gesture, he said, "Yes the same verily sword that I withdrew from my father. Not only that. I went in the night of darkness into Kabuli and went to their great castle and slew the vermin Emperor who killed your grandfather." He thought, *the man's daughter pleaded for her life and I spare it because of her blue ocean eyes... those eyes plague me, now.*

***

As the last course came and went; the three nieces of the High King went to the kitchens and cleaned the lunch platters, plates and other utensils. As the High King sat on the Lion throne, the Magistrate stood looking at the High King and Prisoner X. The High King said, "Magistrate once you received the order to clean Prisoner X who I believe to be innocent is now known to you as my brother. That in itself is a long story, suffice to say that when our mother died, and she told me of my twin brother. I know he did not do it. It is up to you now, Magistrate to reveal the accuser."

The Magistrate looked at his High King and went to him and spoke in a whisper, the one word of a persons' name, "Agrigomortis."

"Magistrate you must get the papers ready and quickly..." the High King started to say.

However, the Magistrate loudly said, "It has been prepared. I weighed my options and I have the papers drawn for you to sign and your knights to get the accuser. I also provide you my severance papers and my last will and testament – in the case of my death."

"Magistrate, I have known you for how many years?"

"My Majestic Majesty, since the day of your ascension to the Lion Throne as High King."

"Twenty years, and in all that time I never asked your name."

"Oh, Majestic Majesty, my name is Cheetah."

"Oh, what a name and it is such a suited name for you. Your service as my Magistrate is very valuable. Well now, send this paper to Lieutenant Knight Panther to command my order to get the retrieval of Agrigomortis, also writ an order of six knights to the protection of the Magistrate."

***

Agrigomortis a thin and tall man has always been behind the scenes of royalty working to disband their type of politics. He had a few players on his side. One was Prisoner X. Agrigomortis knew X's identity, and he use him for every problem he had with the High King. He made sure X was where he was supposed to be. Bold manoeuvring on Agrigomortis part, left X at the deep end to be caught by the Constabulary Knights.

He thought of his informer, the Magistrate's lackey Onarius; whom he waited for, *soon I'll have him, and he'll be my puppet. Onarius had persuaded the Magistrate to become a criminal. Now I have him.*

Meanwhile, Onarius had just found out that he is betrayed by the Magistrate; walking in a casual walk, trying not to look scared by the following knights of the High King, seeing the Magistrate guarded. On entering the inn, Onarius made a quick dash to the side entrance and through the back byways until he was close to Agrigomortis's home to see none followed. What Onarius did not know was the Magistrate had made it possible for the ending of Agrigomortis and his crew of felons; the inn was the first step.

A puffing Onarius knocks on the black door of Agrigomortis, and heard a word and went in, "The Magistrate has betrayed us."

"Onarius, I expected that and you..."

The Knights came in unannounced and followed by the Magistrate who said, "My loyalties is to the High King and both of you are to be taken to the High King in chains."

***

That afternoon for the two nieces of Otto had enjoyed their stories, while Princess Anna dressed in some borrowed clothes from a servant, on her hands and knees cleaning the cell of Prisoner X. On returning to her rooms she quickly undress, bathed and dressed in a green silk gown, she came to see her Uncle and her two younger sisters enjoying their third story. The High King noticed Anna's mood, questioned, "Well, how was your lesson in my dungeons?"

"It was dirtier than the stables." Anna said. She made her nose shrivel up to show how gross it was.

Smiling he said, "Well next time remember who you are talking to when at lunch and at my court. However tonight I will tell the tale of the three princesses. However, we have a few duties to attend to before supper tonight. Come on my naughty nieces, I want silence and obedience for soon you will have another person to harass." *Oh, brother I hope you are prepared for such as these little terrors*, he thought, as he smiled his grin. The girls could not understand their uncle's words.

As the four walked into the throne room, the High King had taken his seat on the Lion Throne. The three princesses took their seats next to their mother and father. As Prisoner X stood, looking cleaner than he had since being in the dungeons, covered in a robe to hide his face from the nobles. A contingent of two sets of knights had come in. Between the two contingents of Knights are the accuser and his lackeys all in chains. Then the Magistrate came with six knights as his protection and the nobles watch the procession; and wondered what was happening.

The Magistrate spoke, "My Majestic Majesty and the Honourable Majesties of Lazuli, the pride of the Lion Throne are at last reunited. Prisoners X, please reveal to all, your identity."

The brown robe and hood, X took off and turned to show all and the hall was all shocked to see a man that look like their highest monarch. Here the High King said, "My people and my honourable nobles I can explain to all. This started more than forty years ago; when we were born. I was first born and proclaimed as first born son and was given title Chief-Lord. Then my brother, my twin brother came next and was hidden by our mother and one young doctor's apprentice. This very apprentice could not have known that the babe he held was a son of Chief-of-Chiefs took my brother to the Isles of the United Legions. Unbeknownst to the apprentice a young child hid to see the death of his father. Scared out of his wits he moved away and learnt law and became a Magistrate whom I called to do his job. He told me all of his life the day I took reign. Then a year later, my mother relayed a message to me on her death. She said that I must find my twin brother, Xavier."

All the time the High King spoke, he had looked at Agrigomortis whom also looked at the High King like a battle was waging, "As the Magistrate went on and became my loyal servant he had to face his own demons when he saw Xavier as do you all."

"I, the Magistrate here by accuse Agrigomortis who kill my father and all the disasters that have occurred to all of Lazuli. I have planned this out to the letter. Agrigomortis, I knew you would come to wreak your madness in the Kingdom of Lazuli. I played the last few months as a fool, to lure you into my trap. Onarius, you did a good job."

The second set of Knights left, as Onarius said, "Well Father it seems my acting did come in handy for you after all."

Smiling wide the Magistrate said, "Your majestic Majesty, I had to play this ruse because I was close to the killer of my father. It was about seven months ago when I mistakenly bumped in this man..." he point to Agrigomortis, "...and apologized as I moved on without knowing who I bumped into. Weeks later did I, remember the man who killed my father. I wanted to capture him and bring him to you singular, but I knew he was a crook and swindle out of anything. My son had been on his last months as a seasoned actor of the Troops of Gillis. I posted a messenger to him and relented that he should return and become my apprentice. When he returns, I told him about his heritage and why I wanted him to be a doctor."

"Oh Father, I came back because I fear I have a son. When you explain why you wanted me back, I could only say yes. But I could not do anything at all if I could see the person who you wanted me to, and I staged a fight in the open with you."

The Magistrate said, "Which enticed the accused, Agrigomortis. With my own plan not out to his Majestic Majesty, I had to play the fool and to make it look like I was actually in trouble with you my Majestic Majesty. But you knew the prisoner X as your brother and felt the truth. I was unable to believe it, until I read my father's own handwritten scroll which I held since that day he died. It said; twins knew each other. They will find each other. I have known but with all the deaths and such my mind forgotten that I was playing a game of cat and mouse. Lucky most of the deaths were stage for you Agrigomortis. My son and his merry band of actors played you well."

The High King said, "Agrigomortis, you are the accuser of this man, but I fear an older crime is more at hand. Do you Magistrate want the pleasure of a duel or would you want a far better punishment than death."

A few moments passed and Agrigomortis spoke, "You are all fools to have me tied up. I have waited for this day."

Laughing he intone a few words, and the chains had slipped off and with his hands he moved, and the chains moved on their own accord. The chains knocked down the Knights. None could have known that except Xavier, who learnt about Agrigomortis's power, could now reveal his power and spoke loudly,

"Agrigomortis, you have power, but you never sensed mine because I have waited for this day as well."

None could not move, for the forces of the two escapes and before them they saw two different lights, one was blue and the other was red. Only the High King moved, and he felt something that he knew it the moment he had all those years when he went to Kabuli. The ocean blue eyes came unbidden to him in his mind eyes, the madness of what everyone saw, soon dispersed to see that the red light had gone. Only the dust remains of Agrigomortis. The High King Otto said, "Hail Xavier brother of the High King."

As the hall erupted, Cheetah looked at the dust remains of Agrigomortis, and said to himself in a prayer, "Thank the God Jorge of Lions, for answering my prayers."

"Father," said Onarius, "let us starts again. For my wife is here, she wants to see you and present to you your grandson Heron."

As the Knights stood, they knew their duty was done and left. As the High King said, "Magistrate you need some rest and look after you family for a while. Next week I need you for some papers to prepare. All may go except my family."

"Xavier, my brother you must stay." The High King said.

"Otto, I can't you are the promised High King of Lazuli and of this land. I must return to the Isles of the United Legion. They need me as their leader."

"Why must you go? Take time to leave. You need some time to recover from..."

"The magic I have just used."

"Yes, it certainly was magic but why it didn't affect me?"

"Because we are one when we are together, that is the power of twins."

The three princesses ran to their other uncle and said in unison, "Another uncle."

Laughing the High King just noticed a woman standing at the door, "Well dear you look just like..."

"Grandma, yes Uncle Otto. Father you must stay, here as long as you want. Mother the Queen of the United Legion has sent me ahead. She knew my love of that actor would undo her. Onarius come on and meet my father..."

"And Grandfather of course." Heron squeaked, "Oh Grandma is coming soon."

***

As the night came and the meals was a bounteous spread, the stories spoken were spoken for days to come as the Queen of the United Legions came to retrieve her husband. As the days and nights passed Otto only memory of the girl with the ocean blue eyes came each night questioning him – why?

As the Magistrate Cheetah and Onarius relationship of father and son become held in their hearts; they adored Heron. Cheetah felt that he now can take life with the knowledge of his son is to be consort to a future queen and knowing his help to free the High King's brother gave him more duties as a Grand Duke. It was five days since the end of Agrigomortis, and Otto dress in the black suit of war and left without any noticing him go.

As always only Heron, the best spy for the Queen of the United Legions followed at a distance. But Otto knew someone following and waited behind a tree which the spy missed because Heron was still scared of the night. Any boy at thirteen would be, and when Otto said, "Well Heron, you followed me. You are good but not yet. Please return and explain to my brother that I have unfinished business in Kabuli."

"Oh Grandpa, you think that would fool father. He already knows what you do and think. The Queen of the United Legions has given you a proposal of joining your kingdom and ours. She is prepared to be under your sovereignty. She understands you as do I..."

"This is a part of my predicament. Heron you may be more than your years, but I am getting older and I must find out why Kabuli has left us in peace for such this long."

"Well then, Grandpa I must come for father's sake." Heron started to walk, "Well Grandpa come on the hour of change comes."

***

It took Otto and Heron to reach the great Castle of the Kabuli and by midnight was in the Emperor's room. Of what was the Emperor's room, now is the Empress's room who sat looking at the window for the longing of that boy to return. As she saw the man with her father's sword come through the window and then another boy, who went to the door and slightly open to see the guards asleep.

Heron whispered, "The Guards are asleep. It is best you both whisper for you both must speak."

"Boy you must be quiet if I must find my question answered." Otto whispered, "You my lady of the blue eyes have haunted me since the day of..."

"...My father's death. So, you have haunted me. Why?"

"My father's death was not completed in battle; the Lazuli God wanted vengeance..."

"I see now. My father was a cruel Emperor and he kept me here locked away from anybody who wanted me as their bride. All these twenty years there is none who could bring me to that safe place as you did that night. That night I swore to have you as my husband."

"Now I know. I too felt love behind those eyes. We must play with our peoples for a year and then we can marry."

"No, the sooner the better."

"Ahem, might I suggest something," whispered Heron, "I have a letter from his Highest Majesty to the Empress of Kabuli in my shirt as a precaution. You see it is a blank paper with your seal your majesty. Now that you have answered each question; then with me as your diplomate for your hand in marriage would benefit both kingdoms."

The two leaders looked at each other and as Heron looked out of the doors the guards are awake and another two were taking positions. He closed slowly and whispered, "New guards and fully clear of mind, we must leave, and I must make myself presentable for the morrow for seeing the Empress."

Otto whispered, "I leave and prepare for my meeting with you on a truce."

Fear of saying anything, she nodded. Heron left from the window and then Otto whispered, "Your Name?"

"Lyandra... and yours?" she asked.

"Otto, my blue eyed lady..." he said.

As she came to the window and see him go down like an acrobat.

*

As the High King Otto returned home and sat on the Lion Throne, he thought of his last night and when Xavier said, "Ah you found love, my brother."

"Yes, thanks to Heron."

"He will make me like an old man with all the worry."

As they spoke, Heron was actually in the Great Castle saying he is an ambassador of the Isles of the United Legions who has just made relations with the Lazuli, "We are here to bring tidings of peace with the Kabuli on behalf of the Lazuli. I have a letter from the High King to the Empress of Kabuli."

The fat footman looks at the small boy and said, "You look like a boy not a man."

"Yes, I may be a boy..." said Heron.

As the Empress said, "Alabama leave the boy ambassador alone. Let the Ambassador of the Isles of the United Legions bring his letter to me."

Over the years since her father she had been a good Empress to her people and if they irked her, she would show how to deal with them – off with their heads. As they discussed last night, she opened the seal to an empty letter. She said, "Would you read this out to all here for they need to understand what is in the contents of this letter."

Clearing his throat, Heron spoke loudly, "To the Empress of Kabuli, may we be forthright in a taming of our heels and I, The High King of Lazuli pronounce what has been done by our parents be no more, on our consciences but for the future of Kabuli and Lazuli as one great Kingdom. May we vent the distance of the past years and be a joining of our hands in a suitable peace. By doing so, I will hope to see you as I am ready to leave my home in the right answer to this truce."

Heron handed the letter back and she saw the words as he said it. She looked at the boy and he winked to her and waited as an official came to see it as the boy said. He nodded and then the Empress said, "It is genuine, Tali."

Tali answered, "Yes, it is."

When she received the letter again the words were gone. When none were around, she said, "You have magic."

"No, your Excellence, it's my magic paper that my father gave me when I need it like this occasion."

The travel to and fro from Lazuli to Kabuli opened trade and such and when the festivities of the marriage of the two kingdoms were such that all could see. The prosperity of the Kingdoms was enjoyed by all.

***

"Well did you enjoy your story and the use of the first time of the Magic Paper, Andra and Otto?" Heron asked.

They said together, "Yes grandpa."

"That is good; now off you go back to learning the etiquette of court life." He said, as he watch his grandchildren went to their lessons, he took out the magic paper and said to himself, "you and I have been to many places and yet more to find."

Before him the paper grow in size and enveloped him to travel to another world.

ROBERT CRISTANTE

***

***

The Dragon King
By
Robert Cristante

Vigilance is the key... The High King thought, as he sat on the Golden Dragon Throne. The Golden Dragon Throne was not some elaborate wooden throne with motifs of dragons; a real dragon, a lifeless dragon, magical constructed into a throne. The High King's conference with the Loyal and the Dukes of The Kingdoms came to be a fruitful event.

***

As the Day of Majority was upon the twin sons of The High King, Darius the Storyteller talking to the twins, "My nephews, thy time is upon thee. One of thee, must choose otherwise your father will have to do it. One of you will be forever envious of the other..."

The first twin said, "Great Uncle, it is not an easy choice. We fear to be apart from each other. We both have been inseparable. We have finished everything together."

"Darius you may be of my namesake. Why have I taught you the stories and histories and prophecies? Because you know how to hold onto the stories, histories and prophecies once you learnt them. Jedamanus knows the law and the sword better than any person does. The choice has been chosen and you both have to accept it."

Darius the first twin said, "It's not as easy to accept it when we know the end. How could you have left you brother and live on as you do."

"My brother and I had no choice like you have, and secondly I live because my brother showed me strength. With strength I understood early on that we must face the tolls of time."

Jedamanus spoke, "Darius, my brother chooses thy choice and be at peace that I love thee as a brother. I hope I can help my father at this time of crisis."

Darius the Storyteller could not help feeling for them both, but he did not show to them the relief of the choice.

***

During the Day of Majority, Darius and Jedamanus came to become men and in a private party in the Hall of the Courts, The High King spoke, "Darius my son, be happy for thee hath come to denounce the throne of the Golden Dragon. For thee hath come to ask my acceptance for being the Storyteller Bard."

Darius only nodded and The High King said, "I give thee all acceptance and my heartfelt thanks, your mother would have love thee all in the things you set out to do."

Alana died of giving birth to a child whom also died some five years ago.

The High King waited patiently for his second twin son to step up to the dais and say the words, "I am thy heir to the throne."

Those words formed on Jedamanus's lips, as Magnus smiled, "My son, you take a long time in accepting the heir-ship. You have been the only one whose power that has been dormant and yet your knowledge out ways many here. Not me of course, for I seen thy power more so than any. Nevertheless, the accepting of that power and the throne is the first step. However, with the loss of my wife, your mother but this day she is happy for she sees you take your rightful place."

The Dukes now the family members and their sons formed twenty years earlier, only one woman, Regina, whom in her sixties spoke, "My what a speech my brother, you have always spoken in that tone since you became High King. And even though you still play the game of life you must renounce that title as the law dictates."

"Dear sister, you jump again to defend a prince of the Kingdoms. You presumed too much and know the title I have will always be mined until I am no longer here or alive. Remember twenty years ago, I had you take the role of Regent and rule well if I were not High King that you would have to anyway by rule of my death."

Paused to see if his sister listens and he continues, "However, my son just accepted the Kingship of the Prophecy of the King. My status is because our father had done the High King Prophecy, because one must have a chief amongst chiefs. My son is to be King of all the lands. He will do so when he takes his rightful place on the Golden Dragon Throne."

Magnus stood and paced a few steps so that Jedamanus could take his rightful place on the dragon throne.

***

To the West of the Kingdoms, five large mountain tips are above the ocean known as the Mountain Archipelago. At certain times where the five mountains tips are exposed a track can be crossed like a land bridge. To traverse that track to the lands, known as the Confederation, to the north called The Four Nations and to the south is an Empire; it is as treacherous as the sea.

In the middle of the Four Nations and the Empire, there is a large mountain, which its top is flattened like a platter as a great plateau. A group of the First Peoples are under some mind control by a dark minion and they were in frenzy. Eyes shone in all colours and only one very fast dragon escaped the frenzy.

The Bronze Dragon moves quickly and with its wings flew very elegant as the sun hits its wings. As it flew, it knew the destination to which he was going. Unlike his other family members, his mind is swiftly apt, and he is fast. With the dragons' power, the Bronze Dragon jumped from safe place to safe place until his brood followed him.

He was a step ahead of his brood and he decided to go to the place where all the Dragons remember as their home.

***

'Ah child you have arrived.' The voice spoke within the mind of Jedamanus. *'You have come to become a man...'*

"Who is speaking?" Jedamanus asks.

'I speak; I am the residue of the Golden Dragon. My power of my magic has waited a long time for thee to come. Soon you'll meet another dragon and he'll teach you the power of the dragons' magic.'

Pauses as he senses Magnus intruding, the Golden Dragon continues, *'you are the rightful King of the Dragons and the King of this land. You are the King of the Dragons you are my son of the moment, and son of the High King. Take what is yours take the power of dragons magic residue take it, become it and thee are my predecessor.'*

Magnus spoke now, *"Take it, and become the Dragon Mage for your powers are awakening."*

Yes, child your father speaks truth he always has...

***

No one was in the Hall of the Courts, only Magnus and Jedamanus sat looking at each other, Magnus said, "I had everyone leave for what was taking place you needed silence. Darius awaits you when you recover from the change. For the moment, I was here to help you. I had known you were to be the one to awaken the Dragon's residues power. I have tried and he would not let me in. But this day you opened it and I had to hear its voice. I am pleased to have thee as a son and heir. Remember one thing, the sword of power that is yours to hold now and until I am ready to use it. Its power is for you to help you control the Dragon's magic that is within you."

"Father, how do you know that I would take my place?" Jedamanus asked.

"You are my son, you have my powers within you, and like your grandfather you remind me of him. He was a father who is just and loyal to all. In addition, you are like your great grandfather as well for he had power even though you could see it in his eyes. My time in this war which we are in is still at a stagnant stage. We are waiting for the next phase of the war because the small victory we had had severally brought the opposing force to recruit their losses."

Jedamanus said, "That is why you say, 'Vigilance is the key'. For the war has been and will be."

Magnus said, "Yes my son it is so. But I fear this is just a beginning."

***

There in its invisible form, the Bronzy Dragon looks at father and son talking, and he saw the changing of the King of the dragons to a human form. The Dragon thought, *the golden dragon known his course. I your son had to follow your orders, but I have failed. Our brethren have gone frenzied by a dark minion. Father, your prophecies has come.*

Jedamanus stood from the throne and said, "I feel something..."

Magnus said, "Come out friend of the first."

The Bronze Dragon came to be visible and they saw the structure of this dragon scales so smooth like that of the Golden Dragon Throne.

"You do not fear me, a son of the Golden Dragon. Prince of my people..."

Magnus said, "We do not for forty years we have been accustomed to your form."

"Yes, the prophecy has said it would be..." the bronze dragon spoke, its low and crackly voice seemed to break, "Man and dragon be one as whole and free us dragons from the hold and sets us free and become again protectors of all races."

Magnus looked at his son and the bronze dragon, but Jedamanus said, "Son of the First People, I know that I was your father but even though the powers in me is starting to seep through my body I know that control is needed. Can you help me in that control?"

Within the mind of Jedamanus, the Bronze Dragon answered *yes*. Jedamanus nodded as he left the hall. The dragons' smile was more like a hungry grin compared to Magnus' smile and said, "Sire you are hungry?"

The dragon only nodded.

***

Jedamanus awoke the next morning, with full power, his senses heighten; he was changing. He dresses quickly to get to the Hall of the Golden Dragon for he knew something was wrong. There he saw his brother crying like a child, ten guards holding his father whose rage and power was coming up to the very tip of madness.

Keep calm child of the dragons, the voice of the golden dragon deep within him said; he slowly moves with a step at a time. With each step, he sees the dead body of his uncle. He raises his arm on his father's shoulder and said, "Father calm down, I must take my place as King."

Magnus furious rage subsided and looks at his son and said, "Ah my son has accepted his place."

"Father, please stand aside, I will fix this."

He walked a few paces to his brother and said, "Darius come brother, come and take hold."

Jedamanus held his hand out, as Darius grabbed it and in it, he felt safe. Jedamanus said, "Go with father, I fear he needs you. Together you both need comfort, go."

Darius left without a word.

There an old man stood dressed in a brown robe and looked at the scene with sadness. The man thought, *ah it seems Magnus's son is in command. My nephew is changed, I feel it. Stronger than he was when he came to me to learn of the church's place in this world.*

"Well Uncle Arlus, you have always had a knack of coming when there is danger." Jedamanus said.

"Aye I do at that. But I have had the senses heighten because of my belief of the God-who-Serves. It seems the prophecy of the old has come true."

"That does not concern me at this precise moment. The sword of power has lost the orb." As Jedamanus said it and pointed to the sword. The guards looked and saw it was no longer there.

Arlus said, "It seems a thief has taken it..."

"Yes, but he was not the one who kill Uncle Darius. A dark minion has killed him. My senses have been heightening. Come forth Son of the Golden Dragon."

Paused as he looked at the guards and said, "Men do not be frightened by the dragon, the first of the peoples. You have been accustomed to the dragon form. You served my father and my grandfather to know the form."

Still they were frightened by the bronze dragon, when it appears next to the Golden Dragon Throne. "Well Sire, you smell the dark minion?" Jedamanus asked.

The Bronze Dragon said, "The dark minion has taken over a jealous human. He has given himself to the dark and evil master. The taint is the same in my brethren. They come here."

"Yes, I feel them." Jedamanus said, "I must find out who the culprit was and find out who stole the orb as well."

Arlus spoke, "Need not to search the thief, for it was a part of the prophecy of the King. The God-who-Serves has proclaimed to me that the orb of the sword of power is not the course you should take. I fear you must stop the frenzy of the first and proclaim it to all that the Dragon King is born."

Smiling his large grin, the Bronze dragon said, "This human speaks true. It is time for us to make you King of Dragons and Humans."

Magnus and Darius heard the words of the dragon and Magnus said, "Jedamanus, to do so as the first has said, is your first task. My friends and Dukes make some room for this day you shall see my powers as the true High King and High Lord Archimage."

The power of will and the magic of his powers, brought every human sense heighten and the two dragons, also sensing had never expected the full force of Magnus's power. To cleanse the blood and bring back the body of Tomas as a whole, was a force not seen in the world. The hundred pieces of Uncle Darius's body in a circumference of a yard; began moving of their own accord, piecing together bone, flesh and skin. The palpable whiteness of the skin then started to burn yet no fire could be seen. Ash burn ash and then a great wind came, that soon ceased with a million upon millions of roses could be smelt.

Fear was felt but not for long as Darius spoke, "For now the Prophecy has come for the true one is born. Neither here nor there for The King of Prophecy shall be ordained by him who is true and the faithful servant of the God-who-Serves."

Then Darius collapses on the tail of the Bronze Dragon, and spoke, "The deeds of many outweigh the one. Truly I bow my head to you my Liege."

The dragon looked at Magnus and said, "I have waited for the true one to be. I have prayed to see him before I die. Soon I will be three thousand years old. And now the age creeps up. I will be coming to you when my time is close to death and you shall have my power. But first my brethren are but minutes away."

Arlus said, "Then let us prepare for the ceremony. It should be now. The Dukes of the Kingdoms is present, the High King is here and I'm here for the God-who-Serves."

He paused and heard a few more people were coming inside with fear, ignoring them, he continues, "Jedamanus here present with the Loyal and the Dukes, are by henceforth be King and Master of the lands of Ducor. Are thee prepared?"

Jedamanus said, "Yes by my strength, power and humbly by the God I serve."

Magnus spoke now, "By my last power, and by my last time in this land. As High King and High Lord Archimage, I pronounce you, The Dragon King."

By magic the sword of power was in Magnus's hand and Jedamanus's shoulders were tapped. From high above none knew was a light shone on him as a dragon like crown floated to the brow of Jedamanus.

***

As the people filed into the castle, the Bronze Dragon had finished witnessing his king being crowned. He is flying above the Great Castle looking at his brethren, in frenzy – flying to the castle of their home. The Bronze Dragon saw twenty-five different coloured dragons flying with red furious eyes honing towards the Great Castle.

The Bronze Dragon disappeared quickly back to the throne room with all the people cheering. As he spoke, "My King, our brethren are moments away; I have no time to teach you all, but I must have you call my father in your mind. His power is all you need he will help you."

Before he could speak, Magnus said, "Son take hold of the Sword of Power, it will control you even though the orb is taken. It has been prepared for you and when the orb is return it will be mine. Not this day for it will be so when it is ready. You are the one to defeat the frenzy of the Dragons – Children of the First."

Magnus given his son the sword, and with it Jedamanus felt within his mind the voice of the Golden Dragon, *Child you are now the Dragon King, feel my power, the Sword of Power controls it. It is time. Listen to me, from the moment you sat on the Golden Dragon Throne, you are changing. Touch the sword to the throne. You will be me and magnificent as a Dragon. It will take time for the change but for now climb on my sons back and ride.*

Jedamanus touched the Golden Dragon throne with the sword, then spoke, "My people be not afraid, for this day we are to return the friends from the first. Dragons and Humans are once again, friends and protectors." In his mind he spoke to the bronze, *I need a ride.*

As he climbed on the dragon, he said, "The time for us to fight is now. Prepare the Great Castle for our friends."

In a moment the Bronze Dragon and the King disappeared, all went out of the Great Castle and there they saw the frenzy dragons coming closer. The three shades of red dragons came first and brought fire. The Bronze Dragon looked on but felt the changing of Jedamanus. He spoke, "I'll take you as high as I can, the change is happening. Your body is changing."

The bronze dragon flew straight up into the clouds, passing the blanket of clouds and the moment of the sun touch Jedamanus, the Bronze Dragon said, "The sun will speed the process the Golden Dragon you will be."

***

Jedamanus felt the hot sun on his human skin, the burning sensation stayed for a small moment, which then flared into a golden light. His dormant and dragon powers combined into a joining of assertiveness, the sword transposed the body of the dragon and the human together forming the Golden Dragon. Jedamanus mind and the Dragon became one connected to appraise itself as both human and dragon.

The Dragon Crown now rest on the brow of the dragon. From that height none saw the change except for Magnus who sits in the triangular room at the topmost of the towers of the Great Castle. He smiles as he witness the change and all the people below were running for their lives. Only did they stop running when they saw the brightest of lights that engulfs the Great Castle.

The golden light was such that even the twenty-five dragons stop to see were these flashes of golden lights appeared from. Darius who stood at the stairs of the castle and saw the Bronze

Dragon speaking to the dragons and with no sound the frenzy dragons only looked at their target.

My people you have return to our home. Bronze spoke.

We destroy those who inhabit our home. The twenty-five spat back.

Nay they are friends. The bronze prayed.

Before the frenzy dragons could say another word, the glint of gold fire came that hit the Bronze Dragon. It did not hurt him, but he felt enrich by it and spoke to his father/Jedamanus's mind, *Do this to those frenzy. Show them humans and dragons to reunite.*

As simple as the breath of Dragons' Fire from a Golden Dragon was enough to bring the frenzy dragons back to themselves. Of moments it did not take and within those few long moments, they were cured.

In the courtyard, Magnus had just arrived to see the Dragons land. Darius spoke, "Father, you help him, did you not?"

"Now Darius, speak not to loud for they know why I help them. Truth will prevail."

Arlus who was behind the door, heard those words and prayer, *which of these two shall I pick as a god. My Lord you hold so much in my knowing that I can't say which or see it.*

Magnus said, "Ah Arlus, my brother, you have age a little, yet you missed the beginning of the new age."

"Nay brother, I have witnessed every detail through the eyes of my God. For that was the prophecy of the old return." Looking into his brother eyes, Arlus read, something he never saw before. He left it unsaid.

***

From the plateau of the great mountain of lands west of the Kingdoms, a dark and evil lord by his very name could make anyone's blood to boil. His second in command a native of the plateau, was forced to follow his dark lord.

Force to help his Dark Lord, Rookus had no choice to use his powers to protect his people. Making a door to where the frenzy dragons were, was easy for Rookus.

"My Lord, the dragons are cured. I lost control. But your plans led them to he you want."

"Excellent, my loyal servant, now, time for my revenge." The Dark Lord said as he enters the door of travel.

***

Magnus sat on a chair and waited for all to return. As he sat in a mock version of the dragon throne, he said, "Jedamanus now is the time for you to prepare for the war. This Great Castle is no more the reigning house. Ducor is your new house. This day, the High King is no more. This house is the house of Arlus. The church of the God-who-Serves is here. I am to live my days here until I no longer feel that I should be here. My sons go forth and are the masters of Nucleor. For destiny has ordained it to be."

With a few clicks of his thumbs, he brought them to Ducor, and he returned to his home.

***

At Lucore Castle, Tomas spoke, "Father has foreseen the future and we must do what he has ask of us all, bring of men and races together to fight the war. We will prevail."

***

As the hours passed in Lucore, Magnus and Arlus were speaking quietly when they saw a wild light. Arlus went and hid, and Magnus just exited the castle. There in the courtyard, the biggest white light, a door opens. There stood a dark shadow and another human form exits and closes the portal door.

The King of Notting
By
Robert Cristante

He wakes up face down on lush green grass. He did feel a little restrictive while turning over on his back. Looking at the canopy of the trees, he deduced it to be between three to four o'clock in the afternoon. *Where am I?* He thought; *I did not go down a rabbit hole... not that I know of.*

Lifting his hands, he sees the sleeves of his shirt, and thought, *is not the shirt I wore today, and even the colour is not the same... this is not good... It is defiantly not a looking glass I went through... this is not earth... to green and clean... but somehow, I have gone through something. What could it be? A time warp... nay it is not...*

He conscientiously knew that he was not on earth, or for that matter, if it is a dream. He pinches himself and slaps his face just to know if this was real. *Damn it man it is real... I am awake;* he thought. As he sits up, he notices quickly that he is wearing a brown robe and is not wearing any shoes.

***

He remembers that he got up this morning with a slight headache. He had his usual pint mug of coffee, got ready for his annual check-up with his doctor. His daily exercise to the doctors' offices was a pleasant walk with his walking stick for balance. As he finished with his doctor, his walking was stop by a friend who was having a coffee and he decided to join him. His talk with his friend was such an enjoyment it deterred the headache. Half an hour later, he went to the chemist to get his prescriptions and then went home for lunch and some rest. By lunchtime, these headaches return as an extreme migraine. The migraine did not relent at all, increased to such levels; he could see a kaleidoscope of patterns and colours, which turns like a roller coaster ride, and then the falling into Blackness, then he blacked out.

***

He sat in a world breathing in the air, fresher than he knew. Still sitting on the green grass his memory was slowly coming back, as he spoke to no one, "Where the hell am I?"

Robert knew he was not in any place that felt like his home. However, something in him seems to remember that he felt he was here before – a déjà vu moment crosses his mind. A keen sense of knowing but a bewildering sense – his senses are heightening. He had no time to discover his senses or feelings, when he heard thunder sounds. He looks up through the trees canopy where the sky managed to show clear clouds. Still the sounds of thunder are coming closer to him. To his left, he sees a clearing and forest. In front of him, he sees a yard of rubble – of what was a road. Behind him is a forest, to his right; he see the opening for escape, if he needed it. Nevertheless, something in him did not want to move. He fears his legs are injured. Before he could wiggle his toes, the clinging sounds came like a dead man with the clanging chains of regrets. He heard them and then the swoosh sound as well. He thought; *I had better try to move my toes...*

As these sounds come together with the thunderclap, he remembers the sound of horses' hooves hitting the ground, which he had played on a computer sound effect. As two

Knights on warhorses bared his escaped, he sees a stagecoach like vehicle driven by four white horses and on either side another two Knights on warhorses. Then behind the stagecoach is another two Knights on warhorses, which Robert sees as the stagecoach turns around – to return from whence they came. Then the six Knights slowly halted next to Robert. As two Knights dismounted their warhorses, they picked Robert up as one said, "Sire, we must leave before the dark of night comes."

Robert could not understand why they called him – **Sire**. A little bewildered, Robert thought, *what these Knights want with me*. These two picked him and transposed him to the stagecoach. As the other four Knights prepared to take their positions in front and behind of the stagecoach, the Knight who spoke was on his warhorse first, the other jumped at a sound coming from the moving bush. A fettered white rabbit just looked up at the Knight for a split second to say something but hops away without a word. This Robert looks, at and thought; *damn this must be a dream*. Yet he pinches himself again for security, he thought, *definitely no dream*.

As he saw the two Knights were besides the coach, he said, "Where are you taking me?"

The Knight on his right spoke, "Sire, back to your castle, of course."

Robert is getting frustrated with the **sire** business. He decided to let it go for now and ask, "Can you tell me why you are taking me there?"

"Sire, it we'll be detrimental to our lives if we discuss in the coming darkness. The Darkness has eyes and ears. We must return to the castle, there you'll know."

Robert gathered that the Knight knew more than he is saying. It was the moment Robert decides not to understand what was happening, and thought; *just go with the pretence of being a sire*. Instead, he decided to think of how he could have come from his bedroom to here. From the sense of falling and waking up in the clearing, he thought; *I have been here. How can I remember being here before?*

Before he knew it, he heard sounds of voices, "Open the gates, the King is return."

The Outer Bailey is a crowded town of people all kneeling down as the coach passed with the six Knights. Robert could not understand why they knelt.

Another command, "Open the gates, the King returns."

Robert still unaware of his title could not understand why he is having a sense of doom. He looks out as the coach's door open, and sees a man in a grey robe and wearing shoes said, "Sire, it's good to see your return. We have waited for you for three days. Come Sire, you need food and rest for your journey seems to be a harrowing experience."

This man turns as a Knight said, "Sire, please follow the Steward. All we'll be revealed, when we are inside."

Robert found out that the Knight who spoke is the Captain General of the King's Guards, all revealed inside, as the Captain General said.

The Chamberlain spoke, "Your Majesty, please sit while I explain to you of why you are here. Please your Majesty; say not a thing for it's a long story which you must remember the reasons why we have called you."

Called me, Robert thought. A voice replied to the comment, *yes called... listen to them... I am coming.*

"Sire, you must eat for your strength is needed." The Steward said.

As Robert ate, the Chamberlain continues, "It started back with our old king about two hundred years ago. He knew his life was no longer like he was, and his call was out to the Land of Notting. This call was for the new King. We are the everlasting. The long life never dies. However, here we are with a King who was dying. He made a call. The allotted call went out; when a man comes with a brown robe is to be the new king. The six Knights you have come back with were to get this man. They return with a babe in hands wearing a brown robe. The Old King looked on the babe and said this is the heir of the Land of Notting. Ten years this babe grew and was crown King but the King's' Brother, Vandistale, wanted the throne. The Old king in his wisdom prepared me his Chamberlain and the Steward with the proper ceremony of the Call. He knew that the Call was more acceptable to one like you. He calls you another time. That time you were here was more as we remembered, and he said that his brother has poisoned him to death. However, your stay was short lived. That was twenty years ago, and in that time Vandistale has wreak havoc on the Land of Notting."

As Robert ate, he listens to the Chamberlain, "Ever since the old king has named you his heir, and crowned you King of Notting, Vandistale has been in search of the Black Cat. This Cat will be the downfall of you and all the Long life Peoples of Notting. There is something else... the Darkness... it is the reason why you are here. We called you to help us."

The eight people stared at Robert who just finished his dinner, and he said, "I thought this was a long story. I see that you are expecting me to do something. But for the life of me I cannot even remember the times I came here..."

The Steward said, "You will in time."

The Chamberlain said, "It is the Call that makes you hesitant to remember the times. The Old King told us that you are from another world with different laws to ours and it makes your body and senses different for a while. I believe a good night sleep may help you, Sire."

The Steward stood and beckon for the King to follow. Robert had not even thought a thing when he stood and followed. He heard the words from the table, "Must we always relate the stories every time we call."

The Chamberlain said, "Yes, it is a must. The old king had made it so. When he can remember on his own then we can stop."

The Steward turns and said, "Sire, I am your personal servant. I have been your servant since the Old King named you heir. I must say you have not age as we have. It must be that you are still young in your world."

"Why have you called me?"

"The reason is you have commanded it to be so. We are yours to command. The king with no shoes is you, my liege."

As he follows the Steward, another heard his thinking; *you are of both worlds... I am coming... Vandistale comes and I am with him.*

Who are you...? Robert thought, then the answer; *the Black Cat, of course.*

By morning, Robert thought he would feel better and back home. However, from the bed he looks at the ceiling with the gilded gold of the old Kings of Notting. All wearing brown robes with no shoes. He studied them and notices the last of the King's with the babe in his hands.

The Steward stood by the door and said, "Sire, I see you noticed the ceiling. Each of the King's was like you from another land and not from Notting. The Last King, which you now know, was a twin to Vandistale was a caring man before the Darkness came. The Last King also told me to tell you this for he knows you for which you were lucky to have lost your twin. The entire Kings have lost their twin. This is how we call you. But those that do not listen we keep the call going until one comes."

"Steward what is your name?"

"Sire, my name is Steward. It has been The Steward when I come of age."

"How can you live a long life?"

"It is simple, but we are not in your world. Here we are the centre of all worlds. When something happens here, another thing happens in any world. We live a long life because we drink the four leaves and being the centre of the universe, which holds the power of long life. We know of your world and all your world does. Put it simply we are the particles of the universe."

Robert's amateur science mind thought; ***God Particle*** *is it truly the truth.*

*We will meet. You'll know soon...*the Black Cat mind-spoke.

As Robert's mind started to drink in the sense of this world, his mind flowed back to the times he was here. The first time he was here was the same moment he had pneumonia at the same time he heard the call. It was very close to his death that he lapsed into the Land of Notting. Once here he seemed to remember the ten years, which was only ten hours while he was out in a hospital bed. Yet a child did not pick the travel through a sickness.

The second time he heard the call was when he had the first migraine headache, which blanked out for at least for five seconds. It was a short-lived travel, but it only took an hour in the Land of Notting.

For each of those visits' he could only understand it was all he had to do to stop the troubles in Notting. Now he has returned, and his senses of power had gained again. More than any of the Peoples of Notting had ever wanted. He looks at The Steward who had noticed the change in the King, "My Liege, you remember?"

"Oh Steward, please say nothing to the others because I want Vandistale not to know it. I want you to return to these rooms and closed the door and return to me within the two hours. I feel it would be a great day and the sooner I get this finish the sooner I can return to my world."

The Steward's head held low in the act that if any would see him it would not go good for the King's' plan. The Steward said, "I leave you to your plans to discuss the coming situation."

As the Steward bowed and moves off to where he came with the King, he decides to hide behind the large vase.

***

Vandistale had passed the Outer Bailey and magically pass the Inner Bailey to stand in front of the thrones' doors. He is carrying the Black Cat statue; he opens the double doors, which made all of the eight in the throne room to see Vandistale come in. Taking his steps, to the throne, Vandistale thought, *a present to the King's downfall will be my gain, my throne to rule Notting;* smiling, "Sire, it is good to see you again, after a long repose."

Smiling he rueful grin, Vandistale dressed in a black and red robe continues, "Well are you not going to take the seat of your power... or you have not remembered..."

The Chamberlain interrupted, "He remembers well enough, Vandistale."

The King of Notting, Robert had just come from his rooms and was about to take his seat when Vandistale made an extravagant entrance. King Robert looks at Vandistale and said, "I remember nothing of the times of coming here... but that is a lovely statue."

"Oh, this little trinket," Vandistale grins, "is not a valuable trinket but it we'll help you to remember..."

Vandistale took a step with each word and not seeing the King's smile, "This little trinket will make you remember."

As Vandistale put the Black Cat statue on the armrest of the throne, Robert looks at the throne chair and the statue and said, "Pardon me Vandistale, I must sit I feel a little unwell." The rouse work as Vandistale had moved away and Robert sat down.

A small moment when the statue of the Cat spoke within Roberts' mind, *well done, you are smarter than Vandistale. I knew you remember everything. How did you convince your steward?*

Robert found it easy to speak with the Cat; *I did it with a command of course. They honour me. I know why Vandistale wants but I fooled him... now you must come forth.*

How do you know? The Cat asks.

It is simple I could not sleep and the book I had left had a story of the Cat.

Ah, the old king planned this all along. He knew his brother. However, I can't understand your part though.

Cat don't play with me.

As Robert touches the statue, a heat from within the statue pulsed. Then the statue cracks open to a blinding light.

Before them, the Black Cat had sat on the King's laps and purrs as Robert stroke the cat's ears. Vandistale angrily said, "You tricked me. You remember everything."

"Oh, come now, you thought, the Black Cat was your ticket to the throne. You are duped, easy. This Black Cat played you as he has for all here." Robert said in his King's' voice. He thought; *wow, I do sound like a king.*

The Black Cat spoke; *you are the rightful King of Notting. You are the one to live here forever. The god particle is all I am. I take many forms. You we'll know now and forever the reasons why you come here. When you no longer live in your world, you shall come to be here, always.*

The Chamberlain said, "It is fantastic to have you back my liege."

As the six Knights regain their senses, they moved around Vandistale and the Captain-General said, "Sire, we have him..."

Before the words came out Vandistale had quickly use the spells of darkness to call his master. From his hands, the dark power forms into dark clouds. The dark clouds were growing and filling as the Lord of Darkness arises. Swirling around Vandistale, like dressing him in darkness – the six Knights come to their King.

As King Robert stood, the Black Cat had stealthily jumped on the armrest of the throne and on the King's' shoulder whispers in the king's ear, "Together we we'll help Vandistale to rid of the darkness. I duped him to save him."

The Cat's voice was similar to his mind voice, which Robert knew and understood his next move, "Vandistale listen to me. The moment of your choice is now. To be the puppet of Darkness or you live like us. Before you speak again, know this, your brother left me a quote – Oh brother of my heart, you are the stone of my heart. Remember me and my love for you, always brothers."

Within Robert's mind the Black Cat said, *excellent choice of words. Now repeat these words aloud, In-far ve'kel-lay do.*

Robert repeated those exact words of the spell, on and on until the light glowed around him.

***

The Steward hides behind the vase which he did not follow his King's' command. He watched the scene and saw what the old king had said to him – ***This is the King of Notting***. Now as the Steward watches, he sees the Black Cat transforming into a bigger cat filled with different colours like a rainbow. As his King and the Black Cat worked together, the rainbow arches to the ceiling and then going to Vandistale.

He heard a very dark two-toned voice speak, "You're the fool Vandistale to have honoured me. I wanted you. I'll have you now..."

"Who do you live for?" King questions as the Steward heard through the laughter of the Lord of Darkness.

The words the Steward heard next were Vandistale, "Sire, I choose to live for my brother."

The Steward hears his King say, "May the light shine in you."

As a small flicker of light within Vandistale's heart explodes, the rainbow light shone on the Lord of Darkness and Vandistale. The power of the light and the rainbow seems to flood the throne room and then a great blinding light flash once. As the throne room came clear, the Steward smiles, as he came close to his King, "Hail my liege; we are long life once again."

The Six Knights getting up from the floor, looks at the Steward, the King of Notting and the Black Cat which sat on the King's' shoulder. They smile as the Chamberlain stood to see his King and said, "Hail indeed. We are all free of Darkness."

The Black Cat mind-spoke, *not at all the Darkness we'll return.*

As the Captain-General see Vandistale stirring said, "You four Knights, stand and help him up and secure him."

"Captain-General, please see the man you know as Vandistale is no more." King Robert said, "Look not on him as a vagrant puppet of the Lord of Darkness. Vandistale is more like he was before the Darkness used him."

The days turn to months as all found their life at peace for a while, Vandistale was getting use of being free from the Darkness.

***

As the King, the Six Knights, and the Black Cat travel to the clearing where it started, King Robert said, "You know it was a funny thing when I sat under that tree I had just awoken from the Call. In addition, each call had a different effect on me. We might as well have some lunch."

In a circle in the clearing, they are eating lunch. The moment Robert spoke again, he knew and felt something was happening, "We must return to the castle, I fear Vandistale, the Chamberlain and the Steward is in trouble." He thought; *my return to my home, forestalled.*

The Black Cat answered, *worry not of home soon you'll be home, remember I call you more than the others.*

What has my family think of me not being home, he thought.

The cat's reply, *they do not know...*

As quickly as they spread the lunch, it also picked with the same quickness. As they mounted their horses, and the king and six knights, gallops fast to the castle. None of the six Knights saw the sky and the dark cloud forming. *Evil has returned*; thought King Robert who looks at the sky. It was forming into a thunderstorm, which the likes the Peoples of Notting never had seen. The Knights then heard the thunder and looked up to see the darkness, as the Captain General said, "We have failed again."

King Robert said, "Nay ye have not. I'm still here. The King of Notting we'll vanquish the Lord of Darkness."

From the distance they travel, they reach the Outer Bailey where the gates were open. Many of the long-lived had died a brutal death. On the path, they needed to return to the castle, headless bodies and heads sprawled like a disjointed puzzle. They heard cries from the ones whom were in their homes, crying and yelling out for their loss. They stay on horseback, slowly manoeuvring over the bodies and heads. They reach the inner gates, which were open wide and Vandistale lying on the ground.

"Get of those horses slowly gentlemen or you'll end up being like the Chamberlain and the Steward."

As the blood drip on the King's' hand, he looks up to see his new friends strung up close to death; as he said, "Do as he demands."

Slowly he dismounted and said, "Who are you?"

"I am the Dark Lords' servant. I watch the fool Vandistale loose power in defeating you. I admired him and even loved him, but father did not."

"Your father is?"

"O be quiet my liege; I'm getting there. You see the problem occurred about hundred years ago when my father and I had a big problem. His problem was vice-versa and I. He made me work in the kitchens. Father didn't know I worship the Lord of Darkness. He did find a reason to disown me and now I have repaid my vengeance to the Chamberlain."

High above the castle there forms the Dark Lord, his two-toned voice said, "My Loyal Servant, speak no more, kill them all."

The Black Cat could not move at all. When the Cat saw Vandistale's mouth moving. However, the Cat did speak in the King's' mind, *Vandistale is using the light magic from his heart. You must open your mind now. You can hear all the People of Notting. They hold the power to vanish the Lord of Darkness. Free your spirit, out of the body for your power.*

Once Robert opens his mind, he then felt the power of the Peoples of Notting. He swam with their life force, all convening into his own power and spirit. Then he heard, "You think not, I have thought of it. You fool. I have prepared for it. Come master take me and be one with me."

The son of the Chamberlain laughed loud, and his laughter could only sound as evil to Robert. However, Robert's love of these people was such that had grown, and his body drop down on the ground. The Kings' body unprotected, the Chamberlains' son uses the dark magic on the King, which had started to break, and pure blood comes out. Not all the Peoples of Notting were there in the physical sense but in spirit, they join their King.

The Black Cat who froze for the most part felt the power of the King and started to move. One paw slowly at a time and when the cat's tail touch the king toes, he grew bigger than the rainbow. The Black Cat grew even bigger than a lion, like an elephant but kept its structure. He looks at the man who was the son of the Chamberlain and ate him in on gulp.

The moment the Chamberlains' son was no more but the Lord of Darkness, did not expect the Black Cat to eat his puppet. When the Chamberlains' son did see, it was too late to escape the mouth of the large cat. With the last power, the Lord of Darkness could not do anything but retreat. The power of the Chamberlain's son could not do anything at all because he knew the end – he would die by eaten by the Black Cat.

The Black Cat then roars loud like a lion and then exploded into the white-gold light none has seen before. Of course, none did see, their spirits could only return to their bodies but all except for the four, the King, Vandistale, The Chamberlain and the Steward. They had the worse injuries. The Captain General and his Knights; those who felt recovered, helps down the two masters of the castle, and bring them to the castle's throne room.

The Black Cat reformed, and none noticed it as it walks out and repaired the headless ones. Those twelve, who had died, returned alive to worship the Black Cat. They told to return to the Temple of the Black Cat. When they followed his order, he returns to the throne room. The Knight General stood tall and saw the four in front of him.

He thought he heard a voice, Leave them, and return in the morning.

"Who said that?" spoke the Captain-General.

Looking around he saw nothing until he looks at the throne, as the Cat spoke, "Yes, I did speak, and you must not say a thing to any. I am your reason for the Land of Notting to be. The King is your responsibility, but you did not lapse at all. Be praise in knowing he is fine, as for these others for I am here to replenish them."

Without a word, but a thought; *I am going crazy*; as he moves out of the throne room and stood guard there.

Vandistale wakes to the voice and knew it as the Black Cat; *you made me ignorant of my true power. Why?*

It was to be. Thus, you know love of your brother that he had installed the day he died. The power open six months ago and now it concludes, and you are one of the Long Lived. You must eat of the four leaves and never lose the thought that you are loved.

As the Black Cat revived The Steward, Vandistale looks on to see the man waking and smiles, "I hope to have saved you, but I was late."

Vandistale starts to cry, as the Steward said, "Cry not and be of smiles for you did save me. I was the steward to your brother before our new Liege, and he said this many times to me, his heart we'll win us freedom." Looking at Vandistale, spoke again,

"He prepared you as he did us all. He gave me the best thing which I kept close to my heart."

With his hand, he retrieves the item from his chest. The item is a locket, which he gave to Vandistale. Looking at the trinket and knew it was his mothers' locket which his father had given to her. He knew it as he hit the little button and it flipped open with two small photos of his father and mother on his right and the left was of him and his brother.

Tears pour from his eyes, as the Steward said, "I thought this will make you happy."

Vandistale said, "These are tears of joy."

Two days later, the Chamberlain revives and looks at the two men talking with the Captain General, "Well, what you all are standing around doing nothing but your Duty."

"Duty is what we are doing for your information." The Steward said, "Even Vandistale has given enough help to last a lifetime or two."

"My son... I should have..." Even before any spoke, he knew he lost him.

Vandistale spoke, "I know not what has happen, but I fear it is not good. However, as you say we have our duty to the King. He is badly injured. We were discussing, if it would be beneficial to give him the four leaves; for him to survive."

Behind them, the Black Cat has transformed again giving a light glow of purple. They turn to see their King and the Cat in a purple glow. Then their King's' body forms a white gold light and shortly disperses. The purple glow change in a white light then disappeared as it came.

The Black Cat sat on the stomach of King Robert and waited. Even the Chamberlain, The Steward, Vandistale and the

Captain-General also waited. Then the gasp for air escapes the King's mouth to breathe and then he normally breathes, as the Captain-General went to the door to call his five Knights.

The Cat slowly went off and sat on the floor, as the king sits up... the hours passes and as King Robert says, goodbyes, he then voice a command, "When I am needed again make sure you make the call less intense as the last time."

He pauses to see their nods, "I have one last thing that I should have done when I left the second time. Vandistale please come and kneel."

He did as bid and waits, "I pronounce to all present that ye be Regent of Notting. That means you are to rule in my stead when I am not here."

None disclaimed it and rejoiced.

The Regent looks at his king and then smiles...

***

King Robert smiles and thought, *I should return home...*

The Black Cat mind-spoke, *Yes... you'll be not at your home. You'll be in hospital again.*

Must I always end there...?

Robert woke to see the beeps of the hospitals monitors. As Robert turns his head to see his doctor, "I'm in hospital again."

"Ah it's good to see you again. Yes, you are...," said the doctor who was looking at Roberts' chart, "you were in a coma-induce state for about six weeks. We had to resuscitate you, thrice. First, when you came to the hospital thanks to your friend. Second time was about two weeks ago and just yesterday you died for about two minutes but came back."

Robert could not speak any more, but the echo of the call came...

We need you...

Two days out of hospital the call came more insistent, Robert thought; *I am ready*. With not much thought, he looks down and sees his feet disappearing. Bit by bit he felt as if he was moving from one world to another. All the while, the Black Cat speaking in his mind, *you took your time to come. We need you and soon the call will be stronger...*

I am on my way and knowing that I come to the call. I remember all...

The mind spirals like a kaleidoscope and Robert hearing the call...

There they stood looking to the door when they heard a voice, "Hail the King with no shoes."

The six Knights of the King's guards, The Steward, Vandistale and the Chamberlain turn to see; from behind the throne comes their King. King Robert said, "How long have I been away this time?"

The Black Cat spoke aloud for the first time to all, "It matters not. The Lord of Darkness returns..."

Biography

He lives in a country town in North Queensland, Australia; where he writes and enjoys every moment of his life.

He is writing a non-fiction story about himself and it is a work in progress.

Currently a Non-Fiction of the Australian Italian Festival – 25th Anniversary special edition published by the Australian Italian Festival and a Short Story published in Specul8 Publishing.

His works had appeared in Pill Hill Press, Wicked East Press and Static Movement which his works are out of print, he is doing a collection of some of those stories title - Just sitting at my desk... Writing.

Check his website https://www[1].robertcristante.com[2] for more information.

And follow the books and movie review site http:// writerrobertcristante.wordpress.com.

---

1.   http://www.robertcristante.com/

2.   http://www.robertcristante.com/

Coming soon from this author

Coming to late 2023

Just sitting at my computer desk... Writing

Coming between 2022 – 2032
The Ducelord Chronicles

Book 1:- The Saga of The Twins Part 1

Coming Soon in 2024

Book 2:-The Saga of The Twins Part 2

Coming Soon in 2026

Book 3:- The High King Highlord Archimage

Coming Soon in 2028

Book 4:- The Dragon King

Coming in 2030

Book 5:- The True One

Coming in 2032

Please note:– The above titles may change as they are working titles. Also the dates shown above may change depending on the author, however please keep a look on his website, www.robertcristante.com.